Hope's Happy Birthday Book Club
Donated By:

Joshua Chen
for his
Birthday :
September 26

To Celebrate a Special Day!
Hope Lutheran Christian School

AUTO-B-GOOD

ATTACK OF THE RUNAWAY ROBOT
A LESSON IN RESPONSIBILITY

WRITTEN BY PHILLIP WALTON

ART BY RISING STAR STUDIOS

Free Activities, Coloring Pages, and Character Building Lessons Available Online!
www.risingstareducation.com

RISINGSTAR
STUDIOS

ATTACK OF THE RUNAWAY ROBOT: A Lesson in Responsibility

Written by Phillip Walton

A story based on the characters from the series Auto-B-Good™

ART & EDITORIAL DIRECTOR
Tom Oswald

CONTRIBUTING EDITOR
Nick Rogosienski

ADDITIONAL EDITING
Colleen Sexton

LEAD 3D ARTIST
Phillip Walton

ADDITIONAL ART
Drew Blom
Bruce Pukema

GRAPHIC DESIGNER AND LETTERER
Steve Plummer

COVER DESIGN
Steve Plummer

PRODUCTION MANAGER
Nick Rogosienski

PRODUCTION COORDINATOR
Mark Nordling

SPECIAL THANKS
John Richards
Linda Bettes
Barbara Gruener
Jack Currier

Printed in China:
Shenzhen Donnelley Printing Co., Ltd
Shenzhen, Guangdong Province, China
Completed: February 2010
P1_0210

Publisher's Cataloging-In-Publication Data
(Prepared by The Donohue Group, Inc.)

Walton, Phillip.
   Attack of the runaway robot : a lesson in responsibility / written by Phillip Walton ; art by Rising Star Studios.
      p. : ill. (holographic) ; cm. -- (Auto-B-Good)

Previously published in 2009.
Summary: A story based on the characters from the video series Auto-B-Good. Izzi gets a lesson in responsibility when her malfunctioning pet robot goes on a rampage through town.
Interest age level: 005-009.
ISBN: 978-1-936086-43-6 (hardcover/library binding)
ISBN: 978-1-936086-49-8 (pbk.)

1. Responsibility--Juvenile fiction. 2. Robots--Juvenile fiction. 3. Responsibility--Fiction. 4. Robots--Fiction. I. Rising Star Studios. II. Title.

PZ7.W3586 At 2010
[E]

2009913118

A tiny robot named OB Jr. whirred and spun happily around Professor's lab.

He zoomed over to his new owner, Izzi.

1

"Well, it looks like you are quite pleased with your birthday present, Izzi," Professor said from his workbench.

"Oh, yes!" Izzi replied. "I never thought having a robot could be so much fun."

"A lot of fun, yes. But also a lot of responsibility," Professor said. "You'll need to care for him and whatever happens, good or bad, OB Jr. is your responsibility."

"Are you sure you can d

Izzi tickled OB Jr. on his metal chin. "Sure, Professor. We're going to have such a good time."

"There's one last thing," Professor added. "You must be sure to bring him inside every night. The morning dew can damage his wiring."

"I think you remember the last time OB Jr.'s circuits were destroyed. He caused quite a stir."

"You have nothing to worry about, Professor. I'll be responsible," Izzi said cheerfully.

"Try this, OB," Izzi called and handed OB Jr. a paintbrush.
First, they painted pictures of each other. Then Izzi taught
OB to spell his name in magnetic letters.

"Having a robot is fun and easy. I don't know what Professor was so worried about," Izzi laughed.

"Hey, Izzi," EJ called from the road. "I'm going to get ice cream. You want to come?"

"Sure!" Izzi shouted and raced forward. A mournful B E E P stopped her.

"Oh, sorry OB," Izzi said. "You can't have ice cream.
But you can stay here and pick up sticks for me."
The robot saluted her and went right to work.

Izzi returned home much later. She was so tired from having fun with EJ that she forgot all about her robot. Meanwhile, OB Jr. kept picking up sticks.

Later that night, the dew began to settle and something inside OB Jr. went **POP**! His little circuits were fried!

Suddenly, the damaged robot began to collect more than just sticks. He grabbed branches, logs, and even some trees. He piled them all in Izzi's driveway. OB Jr. then picked up the paint brush and flew off into the night.

The next morning, when Izzi tried to leave the house, she found her driveway completely blocked. "Look at this mess! What happened?" Izzi wondered.

Izzi drove into the street and looked around.

"Oh, no!" Izzi cried. "OB Jr. painted everything! Why would he do that?"

Izzi suddenly spotted her little robot. "Oh dear! I left OB Jr. outside all night!" Izzi finally realized. "I hope he's OK." But as she looked closely it was clear something was wrong.

BZZT!

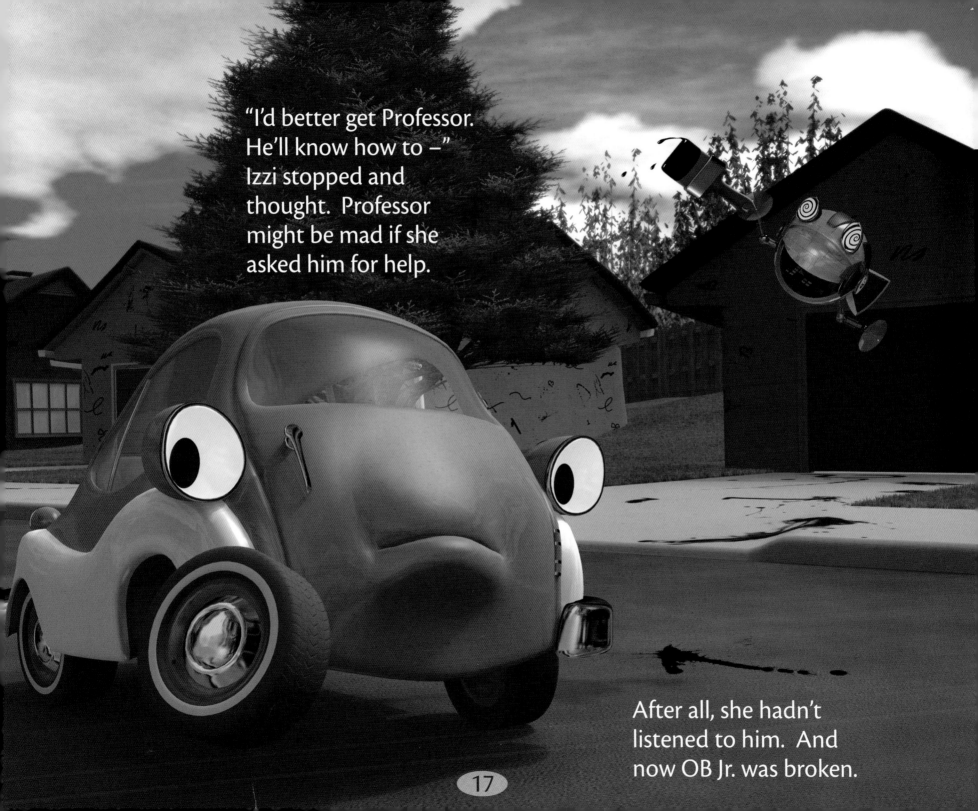

"I'd better get Professor. He'll know how to –" Izzi stopped and thought. Professor might be mad if she asked him for help.

After all, she hadn't listened to him. And now OB Jr. was broken.

Izzi began to panic. "This is all EJ's fault!" she said to herself. "I wouldn't have forgotten about OB Jr. if EJ hadn't asked me to go for ice cream." Izzi dragged OB Jr. back inside her house and locked the door.

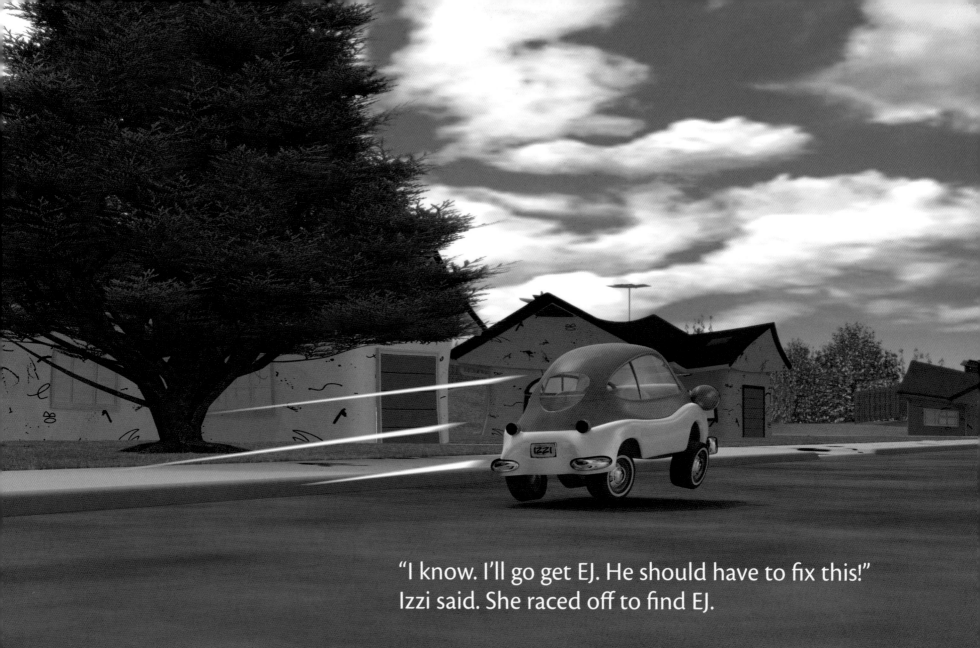

"I know. I'll go get EJ. He should have to fix this!"
Izzi said. She raced off to find EJ.

Inside the house, OB Jr. began to twitch.

19

A short time later, Izzi and EJ returned to her house. They saw that Izzi's window was broken, and OB Jr. was nowhere to be found. "He's gone!" Izzi shrieked. "We have to find him!"

"Shouldn't you ask Professor for help?" EJ asked.

"I can't let Professor know that I wasn't responsible with OB Jr." Izzi cried. "Come on! We have to get OB back before he gets into any more trouble."

Izzi and EJ raced around. It wasn't long before they found OB Jr. "There he is!" EJ shouted. OB Jr. circled slowly. He held a large paintbrush.

"OB?" Izzi asked carefully. "What are you doing?"

"I got him!" EJ shouted and jumped to grab the wayward robot.

23

...OB painted an even bigger mustache and a goatee on her. EJ snorted with laughter.

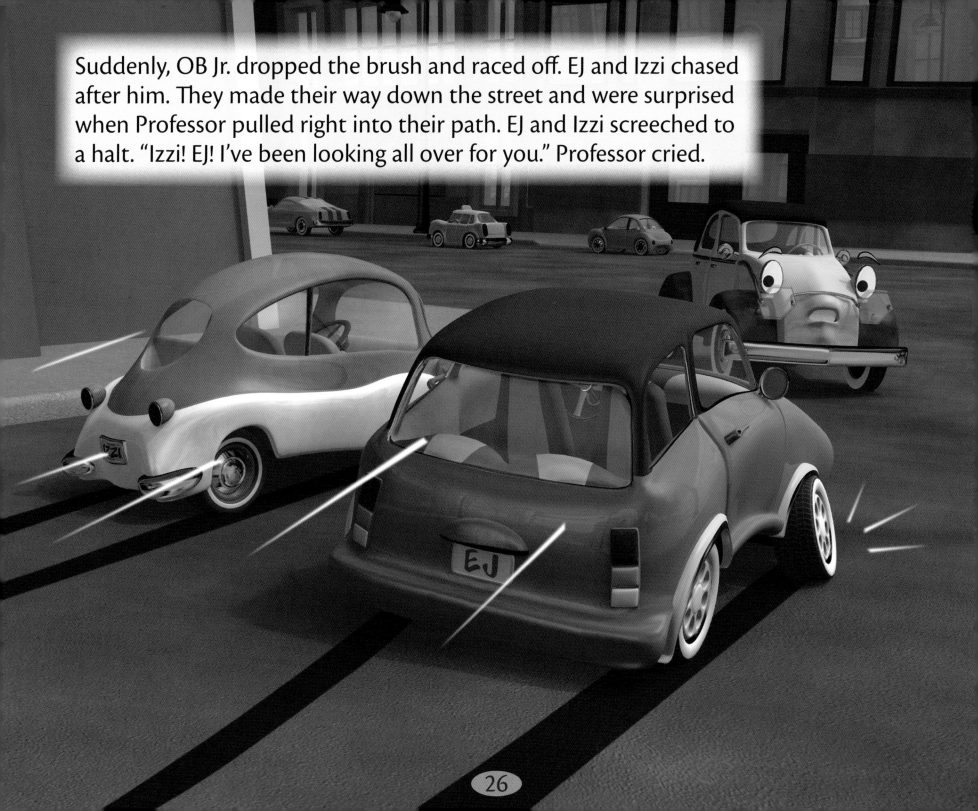

Suddenly, OB Jr. dropped the brush and raced off. EJ and Izzi chased after him. They made their way down the street and were surprised when Professor pulled right into their path. EJ and Izzi screeched to a halt. "Izzi! EJ! I've been looking all over for you." Professor cried.

"Uh, hi Professor," Izzi said uneasily. "What's up?"

"Have you noticed anything strange going on?" Professor asked.

27

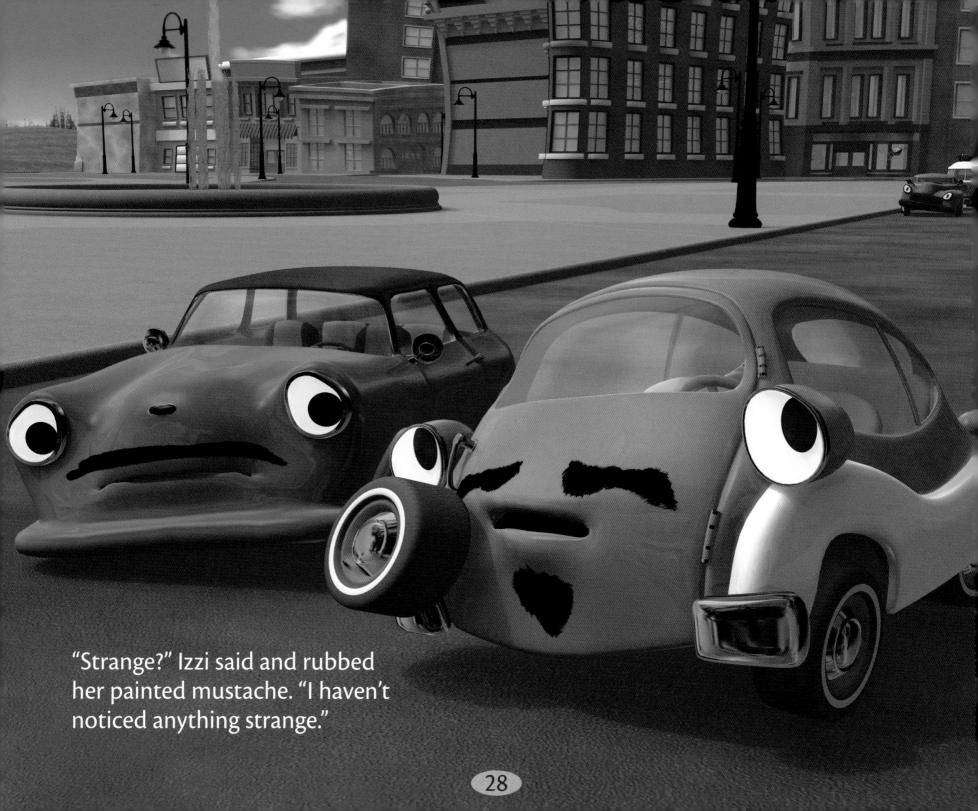

"Strange?" Izzi said and rubbed her painted mustache. "I haven't noticed anything strange."

28

"Someone has been painting the signs. Look!" Professor pointed to a billboard. Izzi shrieked.

JUMPITOL® (boostforotin H₂O)

OB RulZ

POWER *when you need it most!*

"OB Rulz? Do you know anything about this?" Professor asked. "Is there something wrong with OB Jr.?"

"Wrong?" Izzi replied. "No...I certainly didn't leave him out overnight. And he's definitely not broken and running loose around the city..."

31

OB zoomed by and painted a large mustache on Professor. Professor jumped back, startled. "Izzadora..." Professor said sternly.

"OK, I guess I'll tell the truth,"
Izzi sighed.... "It's all *EJ's* fault."

"My fault!" EJ exclaimed.

33

"Or your fault, Professor," Izzi said. "You made OB Jr. so breakable."

Professor had heard enough. He extended his magnet and quickly captured the crazy robot.

34

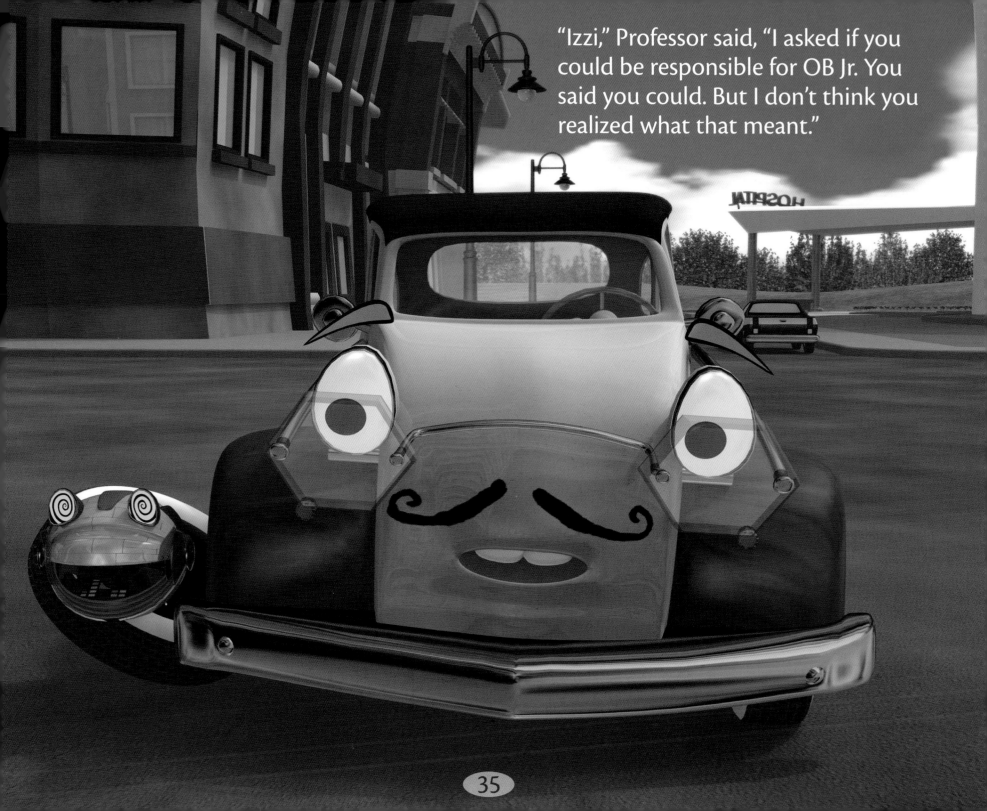

"Izzi," Professor said, "I asked if you could be responsible for OB Jr. You said you could. But I don't think you realized what that meant."

"But I played with him," Izzi stammered. "And... I taught him how to paint... and even to spell his name."

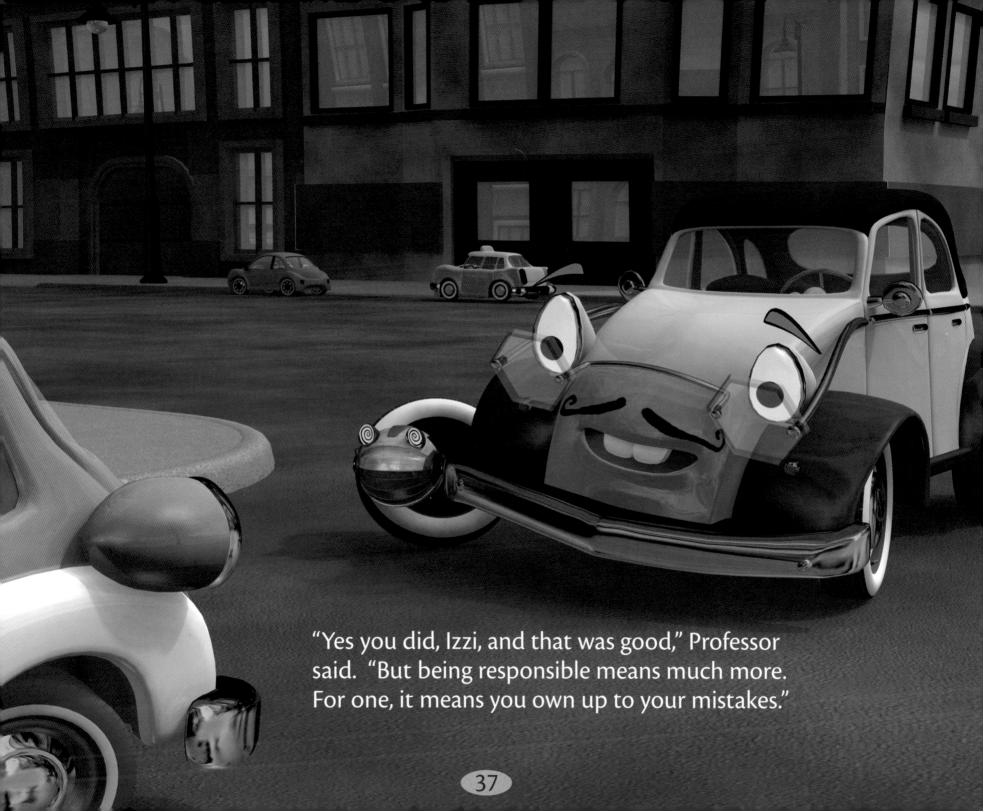

"Yes you did, Izzi, and that was good," Professor said. "But being responsible means much more. For one, it means you own up to your mistakes."

"You're right, Professor," Izzi agreed. "I forgot OB Jr. outside. And when he was out of control, I didn't come to you for help. I suppose it wasn't right to blame EJ either, was it?"

"That is correct," Professor said. "It's very easy to blame others when things go wrong."

"But when they do, you need to do your best to make things right."

"I understand Professor," Izzi said. "I'll do my best to clean up this mess and try to be more responsible from now on."

Professor beamed. "You've learned an important lesson," he said. "We'll get OB Jr. fixed and give you another chance. Responsibility also means you keep on trying to do what's right and not give up."

And so while Professor was fixing the damaged robot, Izzi and EJ spent all week helping clean up the mess that OB Jr. made.

Soon OB Jr. and the neighborhood were back to normal.

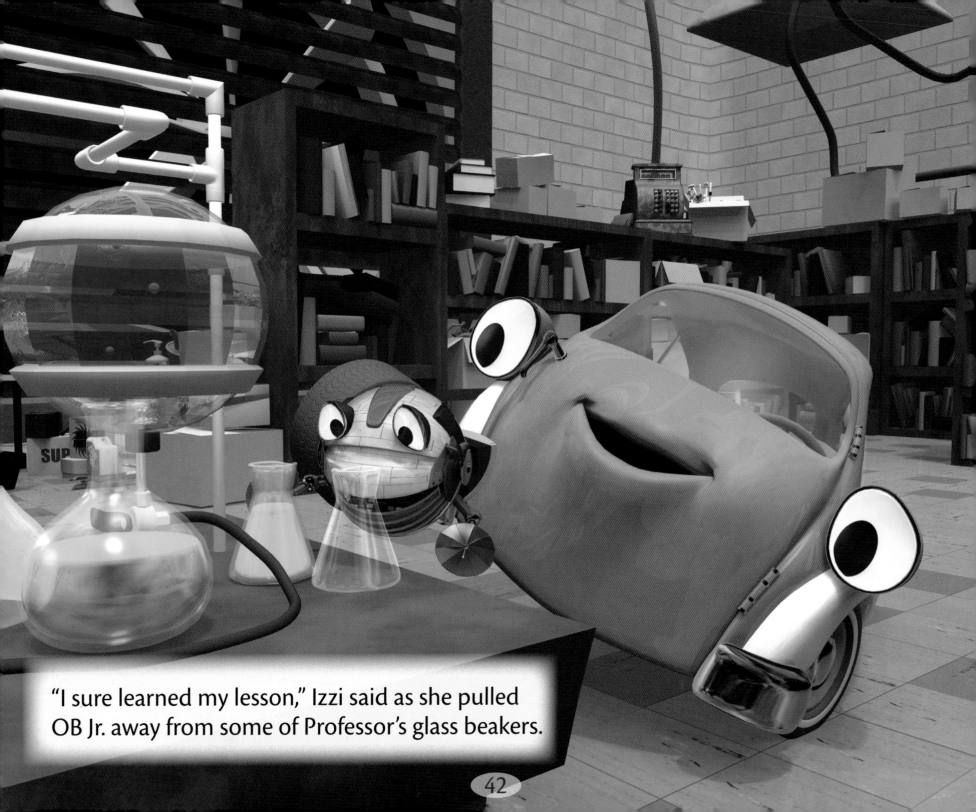

"I sure learned my lesson," Izzi said as she pulled OB Jr. away from some of Professor's glass beakers.

"You know, Professor," Izzi said, "Taking responsibility for OB was a lot bigger job than I thought it would be. But I think I'm getting the hang of it, don't you think so Professor? Uh... Professor?"

Professor turned around. "Oh no!" Izzi gasped. "Did OB Jr. go wild again and paint you?"

"Nothing like that," Professor chuckled. "Actually, I just like the way the mustache looks."

They both laughed and laughed.